COMMUNITY · CONNECTIONS

?

PROJECT TGIF
CHARITIES STARTED BY KIDS!
BY MELISSA SHERMAN PEARL AND DAVID A. SHERMAN

Published in the United States of America by Cherry Lake Publishing
Ann Arbor, Michigan
www.cherrylakepublishing.com

Reading Adviser: Marla Conn MS, Ed., Literacy specialist, Read-Ability, Inc.

Photo Credits: Photos used with permission from Project TGIF, Cover, 1, 7, 9, 11, 13, 15, 17, 19, 21; © Volodymyr Goinyk / Shutterstock.com, 5

LIBRARY OF CONGRESS CATALOGING-IN-PUBLICATION DATA HAS BEEN FILED AND IS AVAILABLE AT CATALOG.LOC.GOV

Cherry Lake Publishing would like to acknowledge the
work of The Partnership for 21st Century Learning. Please
visit *www.p21.org* for more information.

Printed in the United States of America
Corporate Graphics

CONTENTS

HOW DO THEY HELP?

WARM HOMES, COOL EARTH

Global warming is the gradual rise in Earth's temperature. A small increase is enough to lead to polar ice melting and a rise in sea levels. This change impacts coastlines and can endanger plants and animals.

In 2008, a group of fifth graders in Westerly, Rhode Island, was involved with a program that encourages students to work together

According to NASA, Earth's global temperature is 1.7 degrees Fahrenheit hotter than it was in 1880.

Generally a 1.7 degree Fahrenheit change in temperature doesn't make much of a difference—you won't feel any hotter or colder. For water, it can make a big difference. How cold does it have to be for water to freeze? How hot does it have to be for water to boil?

to find creative solutions for world problems. They read a story about families in their town that couldn't afford to heat their homes in winter.

Around the same time, they went to a science expo. There they learned that waste cooking oil (WCO) can be turned into a fuel called **biodiesel**. Using a gallon of biodiesel instead of a gallon of petroleum-based fuel saves 20 pounds (9 kilograms) of carbon dioxide from being released into the **atmosphere**.

Organizations that help families living in poverty rely on donations and funding from other sources.

LOOK!

Biodiesel can be used to heat homes and run diesel engines. Look online or at the library to find more ways biodiesel and other biofuels can be used.

Too much carbon dioxide in the atmosphere adds to global warming.

The team was inspired to tackle the problems of both global warming and keeping people in their community warm. Using instructions found on YouTube, the fifth graders were able to make their own batch of biodiesel. While the team of six couldn't make enough biofuel to support the town, they knew there were companies that could. This is how Project TGIF began.

Cassandra Lin, John Perino, Isaac Kaufman, Taylor Fiore-Chettiar, Miles Temel, and Vanessa Bertsch are the founding members of Project TGIF.

Carbon and oxygen are elements that bind together to form carbon dioxide. Look online or at the library to learn about what creates carbon dioxide.

GREASE IS THE WORD

Research showed the team that restaurants produce between 100 and 300 gallons (378 and 1,135 liters) of WCO per month. These restaurants then pay a company to dispose of the oil. TGIF thought restaurants should donate their oil to be recycled into biodiesel. Then the biodiesel could be sold, and a portion of the **proceeds** could be donated to local charities for their emergency heating programs.

WCO should be placed in bins specifically made for WCO recycling.

COOKING
ONLY!

Some restaurant owners wouldn't even speak with the Project TGIF crew because they were so young. Have you ever had someone not listen to something important you wanted to discuss because of your age? Have your friends? Ask them.

11

Next, they **contracted** with Newport Biodiesel to collect the oil from the restaurants and convert it to biodiesel. From there, the biodiesel would be sold to various companies and individuals.

Raising awareness about their project to get more people involved was important. They handed out flyers at supermarkets and made a radio commercial encouraging people to recycle their WCO.

Once Project TGIF got one local restaurant to sign up for the program, many other restaurants followed.

CREATE!

Project TGIF
handed out flyers
at supermarkets
encouraging people
to recycle their WCO.
Think of something
that inspires you and
create a flyer for it.

13

These young scientists-turned-**philanthropists** saw this project as a chance to change people's recycling habits and maybe some laws, too. They made a presentation to the Town Council in November 2008 to establish a cooking oil recycling container at the Westerly Transfer Station. The transfer station already handled the community's other recycling needs. This container would give people a place to donate and recycle their cooking oil.

Presenting an idea or project to your town council is a good way to start a policy change.

Do you know any restaurant owners in your town? Ask them what they do with their used cooking oil.

In 2011, the student team went to the Rhode Island State House to testify on the Used Cooking Oil Recycling Act. This was a bill that TGIF helped introduce. It would require all businesses to recycle their used cooking oil. The bill went into effect on January 1, 2012. The next month, John and Cassandra were invited to go to the White House Science Fair where they met President Obama.

Both regular citizens and businesses are able to use the Project TGIF recycling containers.

In 6 years, how much BioHeat (a biodiesel blend) do you think Project TGIF has been able to donate? How many families do you think they've helped? If you guessed more than 52,000 gallons and 520 families, you're right!

17

SUSTAINING THE SUSTAINABLE

Currently, Project TGIF's work saves more than 960,000 pounds (435,449 kg) of carbon dioxide from being released into the atmosphere. The program has expanded to keep people warm in Connecticut and Massachusetts.

But TGIF's team of students is now in different colleges. How does the **grassroots** organization keep going?

Project TGIF collects 5,000 gallons (18,927 L) of WCO a month and generates over 48,000 gallons (181,700 L) of biodiesel a year.

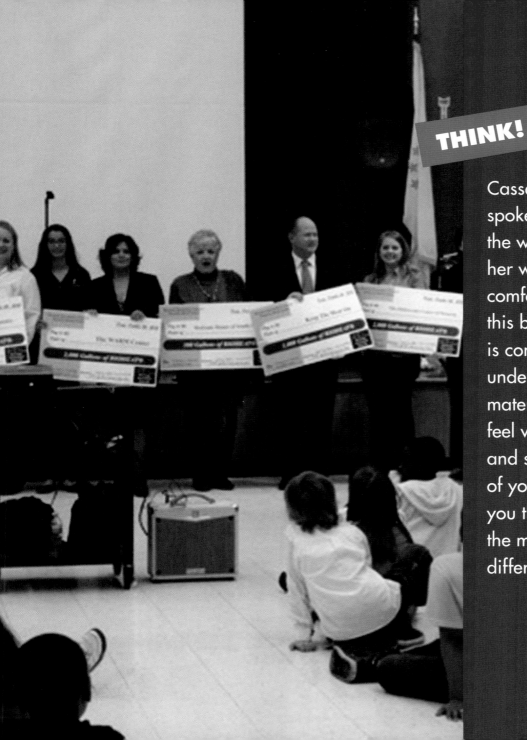

Cassandra Lin has spoken all over the world about her work. She's comfortable doing this because she is confident in her understanding of the material. How do you feel when you get up and speak in front of your class? Do you think knowing the material makes a difference?

The system they designed is self-**sustainable**. The restaurants still produce oil, and Newport Biodiesel still picks it up and converts it. Only now, TGIF is run by the students' families.

It is safe to say that Project TGIF does what it set out to do. It continues to help tackle climate change while keeping local families warm.

The team from Project TGIF is now attending college at different universities across the country.

John Perino feels that their project was successful because he and the team really cared about the environment and keeping people warm in the winter. What do you care most about? Do you have friends who feel the same way?

21

GLOSSARY

atmosphere (AT-muhs-feer) the layer of gases that surround Earth

biodiesel (bye-oh-DEE-zuhl) a clean-burning alternative to petroleum-based diesel

contracted (KAHN-trakt-id) hired for work with a written agreement between two or more parties

grassroots (gras-ROOTS) operating at a basic level

philanthropists (fuh-LAN-thruh-pists) people who work to promote the welfare of others

proceeds (PROH-seedz) money obtained from an event or activity

sustainable (suh-STAY-nuh-buhl) able to be maintained or upheld at a certain level

FIND OUT MORE

WEB SITES

http://climatekids.nasa.gov
Learn more about climate issues.

www.fpspi.org
Read about what the creative students in Future Problem Solving Program International are working on and have achieved.

www.projecttgif.com
Learn more about Project TGIF.

www.w-i-n.ws/index.htm
Read about other projects started by students on teams in the Westerly Innovations Network, where TGIF was formed.

INDEX

24

ABOUT THE AUTHORS

David Sherman and Melissa Sherman Pearl are cousins who understand and appreciate that you don't have to be an adult to make a difference.